Legend of the Ghost Buck

Lane Walker

Hometown Hunters Collection
www.bakkenbooks.com

Revised Edition
Legend of the Ghost Buck by Lane Walker
Copyright © 2014, 2021 Lane Walker

ISBN 978-1-955657-00-6
For Worldwide Distribution
Printed in the U.S.A.

Published by Bakken Books
2021
www.bakkenbooks.com

*To all those who chase
their dreams and keep the faith.
All my love to my family and friends
who continue to support and inspire me.
An extra-special thanks to my wife
and daughters who bring me
constant joy and happiness.
Keep hunting your dreams!*

For more books, check out:

www.bakkenbooks.com

- 1 -

Prologue

The woods were silent…

While everything seemed like it was moving in slow motion, my heart was beating so fast I thought it was going to explode right out of my chest!

I slowly raised my bow and struggled to get to full draw on the monster buck. After all this time, I finally had him in range.

The legendary buck had been a tall tale around Pikesville, but now we all knew the giant was real. Almost too real! Never in my wildest dreams could I have imagined that the mystical buck was more than just a story.

Suddenly an icy, gripping fear took hold of me.

It wasn't something that I could have planned for. It was the kind of fear that only a cold November day in Michigan can instill in a young hunter. It was a strange fear—a fear that almost made me smile. Then a startling thought crept into my mind: *What if I miss? What if I just wound the buck?*

I started to shake. My stomach felt like a tornado as it knotted and twisted. I reached and tried to grab my rangefinder but couldn't.

It felt like a wet fish as it bounced around in my hands. Since I was too shaky to use my rangefinder, I would have to guess on the yardage.

"Calm down, Boone," I slowly whispered to myself.

I carefully lined up my peep sight with my twenty-yard pin. I took one, deep, slow breath and pulled the release, sending my arrow zinging toward the Ghost Buck. Little did I know how that one shot would change my life forever!

-2-

Hunting is my passion.

I can't get enough of it. I read hunting magazines and watch hunting shows on TV all the time. And I am not alone. A lot of people where I live in Michigan enjoy hunting.

Michigan is an outdoorsman's paradise. With lots of inland lakes and the giant Great Lakes to choose from, the fishing is great. There's also a wide variety of species to hunt, including small game, bear, elk, and whitetail deer.

My grandpa is an avid hunter too. Hunting became an obsession for him that started when he was barely old enough to hold a gun. Back then, people hunted to provide food for their families. Money was always tight, so Grandpa started to master his hunting skills on squirrels and other small game animals. As he grew, hunting became a great escape for him from the hard times his family faced. I think it also gave him a sense of worth since he was adding to the family's food stock.

People come from miles around to ask my grandpa questions and pick his brains about hunting because he's an expert. I'm fortunate because I get to relive his stories every time someone visits him in his trophy room when I'm there. This room is filled with mounted bears, deer, and lots of other animals. I used to be afraid to stay with him when I was little because that room scared me so much.

Grandpa once lived in Pikesville near us, but a couple of years ago he moved to a smaller house, but it still has a trophy room. His house is about an hour away, but I still get to see him often.

My dad used to hunt, but he hasn't hunted in a long time even though Grandpa raised him in the woods. They used to spend a lot of time together in the outdoors.

My dad is a businessman and drives to the city every day, about a two-hour drive. Growing up in

Pikesville, he always told himself he'd leave some day and never return. His plan was to graduate from high school and move out of Pikesville forever.

That was before he met my mom—a local girl who always wanted to stay in Pikesville to be close to her family. She won him over, and much to my father's regret, they settled down in their home-town together.

My dad is always busy with work; his cell phone never stops ringing. When he's home, he's always on his computer. He works a lot of late hours, so he does make a lot of money. Dad's famous saying is, "All work and no play will keep the bill collec-tors away."

I also have an older brother, Rex, who's like any typical older brother. We have days when we're bit-ter enemies and days when we're best friends. I'm almost thirteen, and he's sixteen so we're living in different worlds with different interests, but hunt-ing is one passion we share. We both love to hunt!

Then there's my mom. She's a patient and loving woman. I guess you could say that she's the glue that holds our family together. Mom stays at home and supports Dad and us boys. She always has the best advice and is an awesome cook.

The one thing that really bothers me about our family is my relationship with my father. Mom does a good job of covering for Dad when he's not around.

She always says things like "Be patient; he has a lot going on at work," or "Your dad provides us with a nice income, and that allows me to stay home." But there are some things that even Mom can't ignore or disguise.

I'm thankful for Dad's work ethic, but sometimes I think I'd rather live in a smaller house or have less money if it meant Dad would be home more. Or if when he is home, he's actually paying attention to Rex and me and listening to what's going on with us.

I would like to say I have a normal family, but I don't know what normal really is. At least it's *normal* to me. However, everything that I thought was normal and part of the Mason household was about to change forever.

This fall would definitely be a season that everyone in Pikesville would never forget.

-3-

It was early November, and a farmer named Hank Atwater sat down for breakfast at the Main Street Café.

This was nothing out of the ordinary. Hank had just finished harvesting all his crops for the year. Once his crops were all in, he made it a tradition to meet the local crew for breakfast. The Atwaters operate a large farm west of Pikesville. This year the crops had been particularly good. He couldn't remember the last time his corn was so high, and his beans grew so well.

The Main Street Café had its usual patrons. Five men from Hank's crew sat comfortably on the long line of stools at the counter, all laughing and telling stories. That morning started out like every other morning, but it would soon prove to be anything but ordinary.

No one knew that the events from that day would have lasting effects on the entire community. It would drive even the most novice hunters crazy.

That day would go down in Pikesville's history books as the first sighting of a legend. And Mr. Atwater was the first recorded witness.

Gun hunting season was right around the corner, so little Pikesville was starting to fill up with hunters from the city. Many of them sat in the window booths at the crowded café.

The temperature had dropped to a crisp 32°, and the forecast called for a light blanket of snow. Although it was not totally unexpected weather, it was colder than usual.

Hank Atwater was a local icon and our neighbor. His son, Miles, was my best friend so I knew a lot about the family. Hank had been a fifth-generation farmer in Pikesville and knew everyone. He was an honest man but a bit of a storyteller. People around town were all aware that he tended to exaggerate a story.

He'd always say, "I may add or subtract to a story to make it more interesting, but the stories are always true." It wasn't unusual to see kids flock around Hank to hear some of his entertaining tales about farming and life in general.

Hank was a hunter too—not your typical trophy hunter but more of a meat hunter. Their family had a freezer full of venison to prove it. Hank didn't care about the size of the antlers on the bucks that he shot. Most of the time, he shot does and smaller bucks.

Along with a lot of other local farmers, Hank hunted not only for the meat but also to preserve his crops. Whitetail deer can do a lot of damage in the fields. Farmers in our area always complain about the money they lose because of our local deer herd.

But for most folks in Pikesville, hunting was more than just a sport or a means to control the animals—it was a lifestyle. For generations, families have shared great traditions in our small town, and hunting season was always an important part of them.

After having his usual black coffee and wheat toast with butter and grape jam, Hank said his goodbyes to the crew and left a generous tip for Margie, the waitress.

He went out the door of the café and jumped into his red pickup. Hank always bought red trucks. Although his wasn't a new truck, it wasn't old either. Like most other farm trucks, this one had wear from a lot of hard work, but he still loved it.

Hank drove out of town and headed east on Mulberry Creek Road. After about a mile, he turned left on Wilderness Road. His family farm was about a mile down the dead-end road.

There were only three houses on Wilderness Road. Hank's farm, which covered 240 acres, mainly consisted of farm fields with a couple of pockets of hardwood trees.

One of the other two houses on Wilderness Road was my family's house. We owned 46 acres, and I enjoyed every aspect of life in the country.

Our land was almost entirely wooded with beautiful white pine and spruce trees. There were occasional hardwood trees that helped make it a perfect place to hunt. Over the past couple of years, we had cleared two food plots to draw in game. Both of them were about an acre each and the only food source on our property. They were great spots where we could hunt. I couldn't wait to bowhunt the second one, which is located at the back of our property.

I had one special stand that we called the Eiffel Tower because it looked really high. This two-person ladder tree stand in an old oak tree was located directly on a hill overlooking the river on the east edge of our back food plot.

The stand was high but in a perfect location. Deer seemed to funnel through the riverbank and past the stand to get to the food we had growing.

I loved everything about where we lived—almost. There was one major problem for both the Atwaters and our family on Wilderness Road—the other neighbor. The third and final resident of Wilderness Road was a mean old man named Jasper who lived with his dog, Mumbles, in a rundown house. They were inseparable. Jasper took the dog everywhere he went.

Everything about the old man looked beat up and worn out; even his dog showed signs of a rough life. Everyone in Pikesville knew Jasper, and most of the people didn't like him. Residents mostly avoided or ignored him.

Jasper owned 80 acres of some of the best hunting land in the area, and he was very protective of it. He had a trail that went completely around his property. Every day at dawn and at dusk, he could be seen riding down the trail on an old red four-wheeler.

Most people thought he was patrolling his land just to make his neighbors mad. In addition to his daily patrols, he spent a small fortune on "No Hunting" signs.

The bravest and most brazen hunters tried to pay Jasper so they could hunt on his land only to be chased off at gunpoint. Jasper made it clear: no one was ever allowed to step foot on his land!

Everything had seemed pretty normal in our

town for years, but one random buck sighting would change everything. And the three families who lived on Wilderness Road, which included Jasper, would play an important role in the sighting.

-4-

What in the world was that? Hank Atwater asked himself as he slammed on his brakes.

He thought he saw a buck—a monster buck—to the left! It was just a glimpse. *Maybe it was just a mirage,* he thought.

Something big and gray suddenly darted across the road in front of Hank. He instantly slammed on the brakes again.

Then nothing was there. It was gone.

Hank rubbed his eyes and grabbed his binoculars from the dash. *Nothing.* He could see absolutely nothing in all directions.

There wasn't a sign—not even a white tail flicking in the distance. For a split second, Hank started to doubt what he had just seen. He got out of the truck and looked up and down the gravel road for tracks.

Nothing.

I must just have buck fever! Hank laughed at himself.

As he started walking back to the truck, he saw one single track on the left-hand side of the road. It was huge! The track was almost the size of a cow's or a large horse's track. Hank quickly scanned the rest of the road. Nothing.

There must be more tracks. A normal deer couldn't jump the entire road, Hank first thought. *Or could it?*

He slowly walked across the gravel road, looking for any sign of the jumping buck.

"Oh, my…" Hank gasped.

There was his evidence—at least all of the evidence he needed to confirm what he had seen. There on the opposite side of the road was the other track. The deer was so big it had jumped over the entire dirt road!

Hank tried to remember every detail of his

sighting. Seeing deer was nothing new to the seasoned farmer, and he was sure that it was a huge whitetail buck.

It was brownish with a hint of gray, almost like a ghost, he thought. *Surely it can't be the Ghost Buck we've heard about all these years.*

It took Hank a couple minutes to gather his thoughts. He slowly reached for the door handle on his truck as ideas starting racing through his head. He looked up and took one last glimpse down the lonely dirt road.

-5-

Hank jumped back into his truck and raced back toward the Main Street Café. He was hoping all his gathered buddies would still be there talking about the Friday night football game.

Hank finally had his ultimate story—a fantastic tale that was true! He couldn't drive fast enough as he sped toward the café.

Not only had Hank seen something, but whatever he saw was living somewhere down Wilderness Road, right in Pikesville.

It might even live on my farm, he thought. The odds were definitely in his favor since only three families lived on the lightly travelled road.

Suddenly a thought crept into Hank's mind.

Should I tell anyone? Maybe I should just keep my big mouth closed so I can try to hunt this giant myself.

But anyone who knew Hank knew there was no way he could keep something this big a secret. Hank was sure this was just the kind of excitement the little town needed.

Pikesville had once been a busy, industrial town. Though never huge, there used to be plenty of jobs created by two large factories that employed most of the town.

The first was the Simpson Tire Factory, and the second was a lumberyard called Bunyan's Budget Logs.

Unfortunately, the last five years had been brutal for Pikesville.

First, the tire company had closed when a new factory had been built in Mexico. Now the huge tire factory served only as a home for stray cats and dogs. It was a sad sight. The once booming factory had become just an eyesore.

Then a year later a tragic fire burned Bunyan's Lumber to the ground. The fire department didn't stand a chance against the fire. All of the dry logs went up faster than fireworks on the Fourth of July. In a matter of minutes, the fifteen-acre lumberyard was nothing more than a pile of ashes. The once huge logs and raw timber were consumed by the heat of the fire, but it took the embers a long time to completely die out. The fire left all the employees and their families looking for new jobs.

Between both companies, more than 200 jobs were lost. Local residents were left to pick up the pieces. Many of the workers were forced to move out of town to find new jobs, causing several small businesses to close.

The saddest day was when the Dairy Barn was torn down. The ice cream store had been an important part of Pikesville history for more than a hundred years. Although it had survived the Great Depression, it couldn't survive Pikesville's recent run of bad luck.

Thankfully, the soil surrounding Pikesville is rich and fertile. Farming was the main source of income for the remaining families in town. The ones who didn't farm were related to someone who did.

The Atwater Farm happened to be one of the biggest in Pikesville. Hank and his family had provided financial security to the area for generations.

As Hank started to speed back toward the small café, he couldn't help but think of the news cameras and various newspapers and magazines that would venture to Pikesville to cover this giant buck.

He was sure this buck would be the key for new growth that the small town needed. He planned on being the one to deliver the news that the legend about the ghost buck, which had been told to them as children, was real. A buck of this size could change everything.

Hank barreled into the Main Street Café parking lot and jumped from his truck. He left it running in all his excitement as he sprinted into the restaurant.

"There's a ghost in Pikesville!" Hank declared.

The entire café stopped and suddenly became quiet. The silence was finally broken when Wes Smith yelled from the back of the restaurant, "Right, Hank, just like there were UFOs on your property last year. Or there was a treasure map hidden in the attic of your house. We've all heard your crazy stories before!"

Hank instantly spun and stared back at him. "Wes, you can believe what you want. But the legend of the ghost buck that everyone's heard about over the years is true. There is a record book buck in Pikesville, and I saw him! This deer is just what we need to revive our town."

At first people thought that the story was the result of Hank's wild imagination. They all knew that the legendary buck was nicknamed the Ghost Buck because of his elusiveness—it seemed to disappear whenever anyone got close to it. And there was also the fact that his coat was mostly a peculiar gray that started halfway down and continued through its tail. The gray gave the buck the look of a ghostly apparition.

But as Hank continued to describe his encounter with the monster buck, people stopped laughing. With every vivid detail, the townspeople's excitement grew.

-6-

After Hank had told and retold his story and answered all their questions, people looked at one another and nodded. As if with one mind, everyone quickly gathered their things and raced out of the restaurant to look for evidence of the big buck. They drove up and down the back roads, put up trail cameras in likely spots, and did about everything they could do to spot the buck.

Hank stayed away from the restaurant for the next couple of weeks. Normally he was a social man who loved to see people, but this time he wanted to wait until someone else had seen the buck. He was anxious that they would. In his heart he really felt that this deer could help the people of

Pikesville. He loved his hometown and wanted to see it thriving again.

However, there were no more confirmed sightings of the Ghost Buck that month—only stories. Most of them were made up by people only wanting attention or to use them as a way of getting money from the visiting hunters. Every once in a while, somebody who had some credibility shared a story, but nothing ever came of it.

Although no one else besides Hank saw the Ghost Buck that November, Kent Mackwood had a trail cam picture that was intriguing. The picture was really distorted and had been taken at night. When the camera had snapped the picture, it had captured the tail end of a deer. While that's pretty common with most trail cameras, the deer that had been photographed seemed to glow white—almost like a ghost.

Word spread around the county about the big buck; but without any other sightings, the town started to calm down and get ready for the winter.

That sighting happened the last year before I could

start hunting. I viewed hunting as a rite of passage, and mine wouldn't be complete until I got my first buck. Dad always promised me that once I turned thirteen, he would teach me how to hunt. I would be turning thirteen in January, so the next season meant I could finally be out in the woods hunting.

December was finally here. I had only one thing on my Christmas list—a bow! I counted down the days until December 25. When Christmas finally came, I couldn't help but look at each package, hoping it was my bow. There were a couple video games, some hunting DVDs, winter gloves, and a new winter jacket.

I kept looking for that one present that would catapult me into manhood. And I didn't see it.

I actually felt bad for Rex. It seemed like all he received was a bunch of silly stuff like clothes, shoes, and men's cologne. The scary thing was that he seemed happy with them.

We were done opening presents.

No bow.

I tried not to show my disappointment. I didn't

want to seem ungrateful because I appreciated everything.

"Boone, what's the matter, Son?" Dad teased.

"Nothing, I love everything, Dad. I couldn't imagine a better Christmas," I said, lying through my teeth.

"Well, that's good. We have one more gift for each of you."

"Really, where is it?" I asked, hoping against hope.

Dad went around the living room, lifting up cushions and pretending to look behind things.

Finally, he had pity on us and pointed to the door.

"Go ahead, boys. Look in the garage."

I took off. I don't think I ever ran so fast in my life. I spun around the stairs leading outside and lost my balance, crashing to the ground, but I wasn't going to let falling slow me down.

I quickly got up and flung open the door to the garage. Sitting on Dad's workbench was a brand-new compound bow and a dozen arrows. I couldn't believe it. My own bow—my very own bow!

Rex was excited too. Dad and Mom had gotten him a brand-new shotgun for duck hunting. Rex loved to duck hunt.

What a Christmas!

I held the bow in my hand and felt powerful. I felt like a knight in King Arthur's Court, like a warrior—a modern-day warrior.

"Don't shoot yourself!" Rex warned me.

Thanks, big brother! Thanks for the nod of confidence.

"Be thankful you're not a big buck, Rex," I said with a smirk.

That night I could hardly sleep. I just kept staring at my new bow sitting on my dresser. I hadn't even fired an arrow yet, but somehow, I knew I was about to start an incredible adventure.

- 7 -

Not everyone was happy that Christmas night.

Just down the road, Jasper and his dog, Mumbles, were taking their nightly patrol ride. The wind was blowing, and the snow was falling, but that didn't stop the pair from their routine.

Jasper and Mumbles were always together. Maybe they were the only ones that could stand each other. Mumbles was so mean he was usually tied up or on a leash.

My dad told me it was because one day a jogger was running down Wilderness Road, and Mumbles chased the man and bit him. It was an ugly scene! That old dog wouldn't let go of the man. The police were called, and Mumbles was almost taken to the pound even though he was wearing his rabies tag.

The police officers told Jasper that if it happened again, they would be forced to take Mumbles to the dog pound. Losing his only friend was one of Jasper's biggest fears.

While Mumbles didn't like the leash, it almost seemed like he knew that Jasper was using it to protect him. The dog was extremely loyal to the old man.

Mumbles had a low, deep growl that made the hair on the back of your neck stand up. And when he snarled, he showed his dirty yellowed teeth. Most of them were chipped and broken. His unique loud bark could be heard echoing down Wilderness Road every day.

Mumbles hated people, and Jasper seemed to hate people too—only one of the many attributes the pair had in common. In fact, it seemed like Jasper hated everything. He hated paying taxes, warm weather, and baseball. He even hated Girl Scout cookies!

"One of these days, Mumbles, we're going to

get what's coming to us," Jasper growled to his lazy dog.

One of these days would come sooner than later for Jasper.

———

Christmas break was finally over, and we headed back to school. Most of the time it was hard to return to school after a long vacation, but it wasn't the case for me that year.

I couldn't wait to get back because we were going to do science reports in Mr. Potts' class. I was hoping I could do my report on whitetail deer. I had read books and surfed the Internet looking for facts and pictures of deer. I walked into class feeling prepared and excited.

"Welcome back! I hope everyone had a wonderful vacation. Now it's time to get back to work. As you know, this week we are going to start working on our science reports," said Mr. Potts.

Mr. Potts was my seventh-grade science teacher. He was usually nice but was very particular about his class. One of his pet peeves was when kids were talking when he was.

———

"Boring!" whispered Miles Atwater as he leaned across the table.

Even though he was my best friend, he drove me nuts sometimes—especially at school.

"Be quiet, Miles. I'm trying to listen," I said.

Just then Mr. Potts looked over at our table. "Boone, is there something you would like to share with the class?" asked Mr. Potts.

"No, sir, sorry," I said as I glared at Miles.

Miles was holding a balloon that was supposed to be used for a science lab we were working on. He slowly squeezed the balloon under the table and made it sound like someone with a flatulence problem. The sound was so loud and disgusting that everyone burst out in laughter. The worst part was that it sounded like it came from me.

"Well, since you have so much to say this morning, Boone, why don't you head to Mr. Wagner's office? I am sure he would love to hear what you have to say or any smart noises you would like to make."

Mr. Potts wrote a quick note to Mr. Wagner, the principal, and handed it to me to take to the office.

There was no sense in trying to defend myself. It was his word against mine, and obviously his word would win. My new year was definitely not going as planned.

Just when I thought it couldn't get any worse, it did. As I was leaving the room, I overheard Mr. Potts tell Miles that his report would be on white-tail deer. My report ended up being on goats. I hate goats.

After school, I tried to find Miles to thank him for ruining my excitement and getting me into trouble with Mr. Potts.

I noticed a large crowd gathering around the vending machine, and I was sure that was where Miles would be. As I walked up, I heard Miles deep in the story about this monster buck in Pikesville.

"It was so big! They think it might be part elk! Trust me, this buck could be a new world record."

I stood and listened intently to his dad's buck story. I had heard bits and pieces about Hank's story this past November. Some people thought Hank was just being Hank—telling stories.

"That can't be true!" I couldn't resist saying.

The small crowd turned to look at me and then back at Miles.

"Oh, it's true, Boone, I have no doubt. In fact, I plan on hanging him on my wall this fall."

Hearing Miles tell more of the details of his dad's story started to change my thinking about it. That day I made a vow to myself. *If the stories are true, then it's time for Boone Mason to become involved in the hunt for the Ghost Buck.*

But this hunt wouldn't start in the woods. It would start in my mind. The first person I had to convince I could successfully hunt this buck was my biggest critic—myself. I had to believe I could do it.

-8-

That night I couldn't sleep.

Could there really be a huge buck living near our house?

The habitat was perfect. There was food and cover—everything that a big buck likes. But a record-book buck? Pikesville had always been known for having big deer, so maybe, just maybe, there was a world-class deer in our town.

I was intrigued with Miles' story, but the bigger question was a personal one.

Could I be the one to shoot an arrow into this buck?

That question kept haunting me. *If I had a chance at this buck, could I make the shot?* I looked up at the top of my dresser, and the glow of the moonlight illuminated my new bow.

"Hey, Rex, are you sleeping?" I whispered.

"Rex, hey, Rex," I said a little louder.

He was sleeping, so I tossed a pillow at him.

"Wha… What do you want?" Rex groaned.

He slowly sat up and could tell something was on my mind. Even though we had our fights, I knew Rex cared about me. His constantly picking on me drove me nuts, but one thing I liked about him was that he never let anyone else tease me. I really wanted to know what Rex thought of all this talk about the Ghost Buck.

"Have you heard about Hank spotting a huge buck?" I asked timidly.

"Yeah, who hasn't heard those stories? You don't believe them, do you? Boone, don't you think if there was a buck like that around here, we would have seen it by now? I've been hunting for a few years, and I've never seen it," Rex said.

I was quiet for a second. I was trying hard to sound mature. I didn't want Rex to think this was just his little brother having a big dream.

"But what if it's true? What if the legend is true? I could be the one to kill the Ghost Buck. Isn't there a chance that the deer is real?" I asked.

Rex took a deep breath and slowly blew air out of his nose.

"Keep dreaming, little brother," Rex said as he rolled over.

I couldn't get comfortable in my bed. I had a million images running through my head. After ten minutes of tossing and turning, I went over to my bedroom window and looked toward the woods.

A strange feeling came over me. I looked up and saw a falling star. I made a wish before falling asleep. My wish was simple: I needed a sign—a sign that the buck was real.

-9-

I was still staring at the faded outline of my new bow when I looked over at my alarm clock and saw that it read 12:29.

I heard a strange noise outside. I tiptoed to the window and scanned around, looking for whatever had made the noise.

Suddenly I caught movement under the big light by the pole barn and squinted to see a dark shadow. Something was out there, and I wanted to take a closer look. I threw on a jacket and sneakers, grabbed a flashlight, and ran out the door.

I took off through the yard and rounded the corner of the house when I stopped dead. For a split second, I couldn't move. My arms felt heavy, and my legs seemed like they were stuck in cement.

It's the Ghost Buck—the monster himself!

Standing forty yards away, he was even bigger than all the stories made him out to be. I counted at least sixteen points, and his spread was over twenty inches wide. He was majestic!

Surprisingly enough, I wasn't afraid. For seconds we both just stared at each other. I noticed how unusual his hide was. Like the stories, the deer was a unique gray color that gave the buck a ghostly image. I was afraid of most ghost stories, but this was no story anymore—it was real. I was in awe, not just at the size of the deer, but the presence it carried.

Then I saw a flashlight out of the corner of my eye. I looked over my shoulder and saw Jasper and Mumbles standing on the property line. I had finally seen the monster that had been haunting my dreams, and I didn't want them to scare him away.

Suddenly Jasper shouted, "You don't have what it takes to get this buck. All you're going to do is screw it up. You'll miss!"

Then Mumbles starting barking, and it wasn't your average bark. His deep, bellowing bark was a signal, a warning. I turned back to look at the buck, and he was gone. Gone!

I woke up with a jerk and was covered in sweat. My entire t-shirt was soaked. I inhaled a deep breath and sat up in my bed. It was all a dream—really more like a nightmare. Maybe I was drowning in my own self-doubt.

People say dreams are a gateway to your heart. All my thoughts were starting to be consumed with the idea of hunting the Ghost Buck.

Was Rex right? Was Miles just telling some story that his dad had made up? There was only one way to find out. I had to talk to Hank. I had to hear firsthand about the deer.

Thankfully, it was a Saturday morning. There was no way I could sit in class and function with so much on my mind. I had to find out; I needed some answers.

I grabbed the phone and called my friend.

"Hey, Miles. I'm on the way over. Is your dad home?" I asked.

"Oh, hey, Boone. No, he's not. I think he's down at Jasper's place. I don't know why he's talking to that crazy old man. Jasper called and was freaking out about something. He just kept yelling, but I was half asleep," Miles stammered.

"Ahhh, forget it, Miles. I'll call you later."

"Wait, what's going on? You're kind of freaking me out too," Miles said.

"I'll tell you later. Meet me by the old barn around 10 o'clock. I'll explain then."

Did Jasper know about the big buck that was haunting my dreams? What did all this have in common and why did it involve Hank and Jasper? Coincidence? I don't think so. Fate? Maybe.

Jasper's words kept echoing in my head.

"I know you've seen him!"

-10-

"What's going on, Boone? You were sounding crazy on the phone," said Miles when I got to his barn.

I looked around at the old barn, trying to think of a way to talk to Miles about the buck. If he only knew about my nightmare or what was going on in my mind. The Ghost Buck was haunting me day and night.

Miles' story at school had started this whole madness for me. Now I wanted his help to find some hard evidence that a monster buck really did live in Pikesville.

"I need to talk to your dad," I said, ignoring his previous comment.

"I'm not taking another step to help you until I know what's going on."

I thought that was fair, so I told Miles about my dream and how much I wanted to find the buck. I was afraid he'd laugh, but he didn't.

"I hear my dad in the garage. He must have just gotten home. Let's go talk to him."

Miles had made his decision, and we took off toward his house.

Hank was working on his truck when we walked up. There were oil pans and some sort of filter sitting near the truck in the garage. I felt bad bugging Hank, but I wanted more information. I had to know more about the buck and hear what it looked like.

The only thing I had to go on was Miles' story at school and my crazy dream.

Both Miles and I stood silently in the garage. We were waiting for the other to say something.

"Dad, hey, Dad," Miles finally said.

"What, Miles?" Hank replied.

"Can Mason and I talk to you for a minute?"

"Sure, Son, what's going on?"

Miles told his dad about what had happened

at school and how I was now obsessed over the news of the buck. As Hank slid out from under his truck, I could see that he was anxious to tell us his story.

After wiping his hands on a rag, Hank sat down on a bench and shared about the day in November when the giant buck jumped in front of him as he was driving home from the Main Street Café. I could relate to the passion in Hank's voice.

Hank also told us about how much excitement he had first seen in Pikesville after the sighting.

"It's like people forgot about all the hard times and were looking toward a brighter future."

He told us how he had seen strangers patrol the side roads of Pikesville for weeks, looking for a glimpse of the Ghost Buck. The businesses in town had lots of customers for a while and started making money again.

"Life was good for a time. But since weeks have gone by without another confirmed sighting, it seems like the big buck has disappeared—and with it, the hopes I have for Pikesville. "We need to find that buck, Boone—it's here. I know I'm not crazy.

Boys, we all need this buck," Hank finished with a hint of sadness.

After hearing Hank's account, I had no doubt there was a giant buck living in the woods of Pikesville.

When we were leaving the garage, Hank hollered to us before he slid back under his truck. "If you boys go in the woods looking for the buck, be sure to stay clear of Jasper. Mumbles is missing, and he thinks someone has taken the dog to get back at him. He's crazy, so just make sure you stay away from him and off his land."

I didn't know for sure what Jasper was up to, and frankly, I didn't care. Jasper had always disliked everyone, especially his neighbors. He viewed us as enemies, always out to get something from him.

I think in all of my thirteen years I only had two direct encounters with Jasper. The first was five years ago when I was riding my bike down the road, and my chain fell off. Jasper didn't help me. Instead, he started yelling about how much trouble kids are.

The second time was last year when I saw him

at the local gas station. I was walking into the store with my dad when Jasper was leaving. Dad greeted Jasper, and I waved.

Jasper just moaned as we crossed paths near the front door. But seconds later the old man bellowed, "Glad to see you could spend some time with that kid of yours. Surprised you aren't working today in the city."

Dad just shot the old man a stiff smile and went on. As we walked around the store, I kept thinking about what Jasper had said. My dad and I really didn't do too much together. I guess Jasper was right about something.

I felt the hard gravel under my feet as I trudged down Wilderness Road toward my house. It made a gritty sound under my shoes.

On the way home, I came to a frightening conclusion. It seemed like Jasper might have something to do with my pursuit of the Ghost Buck.

-11-

The next day Miles and I had planned to go on a shed antler hunt, looking for some sign of the Ghost Buck. When I woke up, I knew right away that we were going to have a problem.

It had snowed a couple of inches during the night, covering up whatever was laying on the ground. We knew the snow would make it difficult to find a shed of the beast.

This buck was on my mind day and night, and I just had to prove the gray buck was real. It was cold and windy, so I had to think of something to convince Miles to go. I reminded him of how he got me in trouble in school over the animal report and that he owed me a favor. So I won, and he reluctantly set out with me, looking for a glimpse of hope.

We started out on our property because we figured Miles' land would take a lot longer. Our strategy was simple. We were going to start about 100 yards apart and zigzag through our woods. Once we got to the end of one side of the woods, we would turn and go back following the same pattern.

I looked over at Miles and saw him drawing in the snow with a tree branch. Although he didn't seem very interested in searching for shed antlers, I didn't say anything and kept sweeping the ground, looking for some evidence of the Ghost Buck.

We jumped a couple of rabbits, but that was the only thing we saw on our first pass through the woods. We passed by all my family's tree stands that my brother and I had named—the Hotel, the Snack Shack, and finally my favorite, the Eiffel Tower. Rex and I always had fun naming them, and Mom appreciated our letting her know which one we would be using.

The temperature was starting to drop, and the wind was blowing from the north, making it even more frigid.

Miles stopped and turned toward me, and I already knew what he was thinking.

"Boone, I think I'm going to go home. This is a waste of time. We're never going to find his antlers. There's just too much land to cover."

I couldn't believe it. We had only been out there for an hour, and Miles was ready to go home. I had waited months for this day—the day that was going to provide me with evidence of the crafty buck. There was no way I was quitting until I had some proof that the buck was in Pikesville.

"Come on, Miles. We just started. Let's give it a little more time; I think his sheds are out here somewhere," I quickly said.

Miles started to break apart the stick and toss the pieces in the snow.

"I'm not saying the buck doesn't exist or anything like that, Boone. But what are the chances of us finding his sheds? Slim to none, and I want to go home and get something to eat."

Suddenly I saw something out of the corner of my eye.

"Miles, what's that?"

-12-

"I don't see anything," said Miles, looking at me funny.

I knew he thought I was just saying I saw something to keep him from going back home. I remember my parents would do that on really long drives. They would tell me we were really close or almost there when we weren't. But I wasn't just saying it. I really had seen something. A couple hundred yards away I saw something moving again, and it definitely wasn't a rabbit or some other small game.

It was much bigger. A slow chill started to creep up my spine and a tingle went down my neck. Whatever animal it was, it was right near the border of our property and Jasper's!

We quickly headed toward it, but I wasn't paying attention to where we were. Suddenly I realized we were almost on Jasper's property. No one went on Jasper's land—ever!

I shook off my fear of Jasper to get closer to the animal. What we saw horrified us. It was Mumbles, and his mouth was stained red and covered in blood. He was snarling and growling. It seemed like he was trying to lurch in our direction, but something was holding him back.

We instantly froze, not knowing what to do next.

"I say we run home and act like this never happened," suggested Miles. And in that split second, I actually tended to agree with him.

We both stood silently and stared. I slowly got closer to take a better look at Mumbles. He was known for attacking anyone who got in his way. Even though Mumbles was doing his share of barking and growling at us, he hadn't gotten any nearer.

I took a couple more steps toward him. Slowly and carefully, one step at a time, I inched closer and closer to the dog. That's when I saw he was entangled in some wire.

An old, barbed-wire fence had once separated the two property lines years ago. Every once in a while, we would run across some old piece of wire or an old post left over from that time. Somehow Mumbles had found a way to get wrapped up in some of the rusty wire.

I took a deep breath and turned to Miles. "We can't leave him, Miles. It's just not right," I finally said. I knew we had to at least try to help.

"What are you thinking? Do you want to die?" Miles shouted at me.

I crouched down to examine Mumbles. "His front two paws are bleeding pretty badly," I said.

I knew we didn't have a lot of time. The dog was in pain and must have already lost a lot of blood.

I looked at Miles and said, "Go grab that stick over there and bring it here. We have to do something!"

Miles paused for a second and then shaking his head, he reluctantly got the stick and brought it over.

I could tell right away that this was going to be tough. Barbed wire is really hard to untangle, especially when it's rusty.

I had never thought, not even in my wildest dreams, that I would ever do anything to help this dog. But I felt like my duty was to try to rescue Mumbles.

Mumbles had stopped barking and was now silent. He was just looking up at the sky with a blank stare. It was almost like the dog knew we were going to try to help him.

-13-

I took off my gloves to stroke Mumbles' head. I knew the dog was capable of taking off one of my fingers with a quick bite, but there wasn't time to worry about myself. The dog needed help, and he needed it now!

I reached down and pretty easily pulled out his front right paw from the wire. It was only twisted once in the rusted coil. But it would take much more skill to free his other paw.

I took the stick that Miles had found and slowly wedged it in between the dog's paw and the barbed wire. I made about an inch of clearance, and that seemed to give Mumbles a little relief. I reached down and slowly started to untwist the wire.

It was a terrible mess—worse than any shoelace knot I'd ever seen. After about two or three minutes of turning and twisting, I finally freed the injured dog.

Mumbles took a couple of steps and fell. He slowly got back up only to fall over again. Mumbles had several deep cuts that were bleeding. Both paws were badly damaged, and Mumbles wouldn't let me touch them now that they had been freed from the wire. He had lost a lot of blood and was weak. I knew he couldn't stand on his own. He tried once again and fell flat on his face in the snow.

"Now what are we going to do?" Miles asked.

"I don't know. But I do know we can't leave him here."

With that I said a little prayer, "Lord, please help this injured dog," and I reached down to pick up my former enemy. I could feel the dog's warm blood trickling down my arms as my heart started to beat faster and faster. I cradled him like a newborn baby and started walking toward Jasper's house, right through the middle of his property.

"You're crazy. I'm going home!" yelled Miles.

I turned to reason with him, but all I saw was the back of his coat as he sprinted away. There I was, alone, unarmed, and trespassing on enemy territory. What a terrible mess I was in!

Just then, I looked up and saw my prize.

-14-

I was about halfway to Jasper's house when I spotted it. At first it just looked like a small tree, but that didn't seem right.

The newly fallen snow couldn't even hide the treasure. I was looking at a deer antler and not just any antler! A huge antler was sticking out of the snow about fifty yards in front of me. It almost glowed in the sunlight, as if the antler wanted to be found. As I approached, I knew instantly whose antler it was. I had finally found the evidence I needed!

The fear of going to Jasper's house took a back seat to the excitement of finding the buck's shed. I had seen a lot of big antlers but nothing like this. I gently set Mumbles down and pulled the antler out of the snow. It had six points and a huge five-inch drop tine.

I wasn't sure how long the tines were, but I knew they were really long. I remember catching a ten-inch bass last summer, and all these tines were longer than the bass. I found myself mesmerized as I examined the shed.

Mumbles' subtle whimper brought me quickly back to reality. The way I saw it, I only had two choices.

If I took the antler with me to Jasper's, I knew there was no way Jasper would let me keep it. The second option was to leave it. *How can I leave something I have tried so hard to find—something that really found me?*

Then a third option crept into my mind, and I decided to take it. I leaned the huge shed against a giant oak tree and picked up Mumbles again.

I trudged with him in my arms through some thick evergreen trees that separated the big woods from Jasper's house. As I cleared the trees, I could see the lights of Jasper's house.

"I guess there's no turning back now, boy," I whispered to Mumbles.

I started to shake as I walked up the steps to the old house. It took all the courage I could muster to knock on the door. After three loud knocks, I heard some movement from inside the house.

The door creaked open.

I thought I was prepared for anything, but I was wrong. Dead wrong!

-15-

I was staring down the barrel of a gun that stuck out of the doorway. I was paralyzed; I couldn't move. It felt like I was stuck in quicksand.

I heard an old, grizzled voice from inside ask, "You got a death wish, boy?"

"I...I...I...fo...found your dog," I stuttered.

I stepped from the shadows into the light on the porch to show what I had carried through the snow.

"Mumbles! Oh, my sweet Mumbles!" cried Jasper.

The old man put down the gun and hugged his dog. He saw the blood on Mumbles' paws.

"What did you do, boy?" Jasper howled.

I started to explain to Jasper how I had found Mumbles caught in the barbed-wire fence.

"So you carried him all the way to my house?"

I nodded.

"That was mighty nice of you, young fella. You're the Mason boy, right?" Jasper relented.

"Yes, sir," I responded.

"Thanks for saving my dog. You know there ain't no reward or nothing," Jasper quickly added.

"Reward? I don't need a reward. I just thought I'd help," I quietly said.

"You better get running along home before your parents worry about you," Jasper told me.

I was relieved that he had let me go, and I started walking back toward the woods—back toward my hidden treasure.

"Where do you think you're going?" Jasper yelled across the yard.

"Home," I shouted back.

I could tell he was getting very uncomfortable, and I couldn't figure out why.

"I can drop you off. There ain't no reason to go tramping through my woods," he offered.

I had a really good reason, but I couldn't tell Jasper. I had to think fast. I knew this was the first and probably the last time anyone had ever set foot on Jasper's property. I had worked too hard to leave the only evidence of the Ghost Buck in his woods.

"I dropped my gloves somewhere in the woods. They're really special gloves; I just got them for Christmas," I said, pleading silently that he would agree.

Jasper stood quiet for a minute.

"After you find your gloves, you better go straight home. I better never catch you on my property again," he ordered, slamming the door.

I kept looking over my shoulder as I walked into his woods.

I was telling the truth. I had forgotten my gloves, but that wasn't the real reason I had to go back. I had to grab the antler shed. I knew that everyone, including Rex, would have to believe me about the Ghost Buck if I showed them the antler.

It was easy to find my way back as I followed my own tracks through the snow. I quickly found the unusual tree and my prize still sitting against it. As I held it, I felt like a king—like a hero.

Then I heard an unmistakable sound that was all too familiar. At first it was faint, but it started to get louder. I instantly knew what it was.

It was Jasper's four-wheeler, and it was headed right toward me!

-16-

I heard a crash as he plowed over a downed tree limb, and to my right, I saw a number of deer carefully watching the ATV. I didn't have time to waste, so I grabbed the antler and ran as fast as I could. I ran right past the bloody snow where I had freed Mumbles.

I felt like a running back ducking under trees and racing through the snow, but there was no way I was going to fumble the antler. After passing the property line, I quickly dove behind some bushes to hide, praying the old man wouldn't see me, or even worse, know the antler was missing. I stayed there for what seemed like hours, but it was probably only a minute or two.

Finally, Jasper stopped the four-wheeler on the property line right at the spot where the dog had been caught in the old fence wire.

Jasper cried aloud, "Stupid old dog, you almost ruined it!" He jumped back on his ATV and drove cautiously along the property line like he was looking for something.

A million thoughts ran through my head. *Was he looking for me? Did he know I took the antler?*

Then everything began falling into place. I suddenly understood that Jasper was looking for something, but it wasn't the antler. *He's looking for the Ghost Buck. He has to be!*

As Jasper continue to circle the property, he spotted the group of deer and quickly drove toward them, yelling and trying to push them farther onto his property, not allowing them to cross onto ours.

Evidently all those times that Jasper had driven his four-wheeler around the property, it wasn't to keep people out—it was to keep something in.

Just when I thought I was finally figuring everything out, I had a horrible feeling—one that was terrible—even worse than fear itself. I felt guilt. Whether or not I liked it, I was a thief. I had stolen that antler from Jasper's property, and it was wrong. I started to rationalize in my mind all the reasons why it was okay.

Jasper is so mean. I deserve it. It's not his. I'm the one who found it.

Every time I came up with a new reason why what I did was okay, my conscience always brought me back to reality. I had stolen that antler from Jasper's property.

To make matters worse, as soon as I showed people my incredible find, I knew their first question would be: "Where did you find it?"

What will I do then? Lie? Then I would be both a thief and a liar.

After all the months of anticipation and excitement searching for evidence of the Ghost Buck, all my thoughts were now centered on getting rid of the antler. I couldn't take it back to Jasper right now. I was too afraid he would not be in the mood to be forgiving, but I had to come up with a plan to return the shed to him.

I dragged the massive antler behind me, and when I got home, I hid it under a blanket at the back of my closet.

After thinking about it for a while, I finally decided on a plan. I'd leave the antler there until nighttime. I'd need the cover of night for my plan to work.

Even then returning it was a big risk, but a risk I knew I had to take. I was going to go back to Jasper's house under the cover of darkness and leave the antler on his front porch.

-17-

Dinner was quiet that night. Dad was still at work when the three of us sat down for supper. Mom had made one of my favorite dishes, meatloaf. Usually, I scarfed down her meatloaf but not tonight. I just took my fork and swirled it around in the mashed potatoes.

We had just finished when the doorbell rang. Rex jumped up and hurried to the front door. It was Hank and Miles.

"Mason, you're not going to believe what we found!" Miles yelled as the door swung open. They both walked into the house, and I could tell that this was no ordinary visit.

Miles' right hand was shaking, and that only

happens when he's overly excited. Hank reached behind his back and pulled out a giant antler.

For a split second, I thought they had found the shed that I'd hidden at the back of my closet. I could tell it was an exact match to the one I'd found. It was every inch as big and sported the same double drop tine!

"Dad found it in back of the cornfield today. Can you believe it? This proves the Ghost Buck is real, and he still lives around here," maintained Miles.

Hank added, "Mason, it's true. I found his antler. This shed is proof that what I saw was real. It's going to change everything around this sleepy little town. The best part is the Ghost Buck is still alive and living somewhere in Pikesville!"

I was both excited and relieved at the same time. I realized that we could all talk about the buck now, and everyone would know that he's real. I didn't have to keep the secret anymore and thankfully didn't need the antler I'd taken from Jasper's place earlier in the day.

The Atwaters had brought a digital camera with

them and wanted a picture of all three of us with the gigantic antler. We stood by the stone fireplace in our front room, posing with the buck's shed.

Hank was in the middle, and Miles and I were on both sides. The antler was big enough for all three of us to hold it for the picture.

"Smile," Mom said.

I had heard those familiar words a thousand times for so many pictures, but they seemed different this time. I laughed. *How could I not smile?* We were holding a piece of Pikesville history. After Mom had taken a bunch of pictures with our camera, Hank handed her his camera. Mom took some more pictures before giving it back to Hank. I thanked them for showing me. I hoped they wouldn't leave before Dad got home so he could see them and their trophy.

"What time will Dad be home?" I asked my mom.

"He's working late again, honey," Mom replied.

Of course he was.

We talked for a while, all sharing memories of looking for the Ghost Buck.

I winced when Hank finally said, "Well, we got to get going. We'll see you later."

Watching them go out the door together made me kind of jealous. I wished my dad could have seen the antler and been in the picture with me like Hank was with Miles. There were a lot of times I wished my dad was simply around.

But I couldn't worry about that now. I had a busy night ahead of me. The real action was going to take place once everyone was asleep. I was actually looking forward to going to my room tonight.

Dad eventually got home just as I was brushing my teeth.

"Hey, Son. How was your day?" asked Dad.

"Good, just a regular day," I said.

"Did anything exciting happen while I was at work?" Dad asked.

"Nope, just a regular day," I responded, deciding not to share the story with him about Hank and Miles finding the antler. He hadn't made it home in time to see them, so I wouldn't go out of my way to let him know about it.

And I surely wasn't going to tell him about

Jasper, or the giant shed antler I had taken. *Why should I?* He wouldn't understand anyway and would probably get mad at me for taking something of Jasper's. I was on my own.

After Dad said goodnight, I laid in bed and stared out the window toward Jasper's house. I could see his lights go off in the distance and waited another ten minutes just to make sure. I went to the closet and uncovered the antler. It was huge, and I had trouble getting it out of there. It kept catching on the hanging clothes.

Finally getting out the antler, I put on my heavy jacket and tiptoed down the hall and out the front door with it. I decided to walk down the edge of the road because I thought it would be safer and faster. I stopped in front of Jasper's and took one last look before stepping onto his property.

Then I heard an animal heading right toward me.

-18-

It was Mumbles! He was limping toward me as quickly as he could go. *Will he remember me or will he decide I was an intruder and try to bite me?*

When he reached me, he jumped up, and the impact of the huge dog knocked me down, and we were on the ground together. He quickly began licking me and wagging his tail. When I sat up, he rolled over, and I scratched his belly and whispered to my newfound friend.

"Just lie here and be quiet, buddy. This will only take a minute," I told him.

I started creeping toward Jasper's front porch, dragging the antler behind me. Even though it was freezing outside, sweat started to pour down my face. With every step I took closer to Jasper's door, my stomach turned in nervous knots.

My plan was simple. I was going to sneak up and put the antler against the house near the front door and run fast—very fast. When I placed the shed near the door, everything was going as planned until I heard a noise behind me.

I quickly turned and saw an old truck pulling into the driveway. *Jasper!* He hadn't gone to sleep—he'd just left the house!

I froze. There was nothing I could do. I was boxed in. He slammed the truck in park and jumped out.

"Whatcha think you're doing, kid?" yelled Jasper.

I thought about running but wondered if he would shoot me in the back. He stomped up the stairs and demanded again, "I said what do you think you're doing? This is private property!"

I backed up and bumped into the antler, which fell, making a loud clunking noise. It quickly caught Jasper's eye, and his focus shifted to the huge shed. He picked it up and examined it carefully.

"Where did you find this, boy?"

I told him that I had found it when I was helping Mumbles get untangled from the wire fence. He wanted to know the exact location, so I described the nearby unique oak tree.

He smiled. It was the first time I'd ever seen him smile.

"Promise me you won't tell anyone about this antler," Jasper commanded me.

"I haven't told anyone yet, but—."

Jasper interrupted when I tried to tell him about Hank and Miles' new find.

"And you won't! It would be in the best interests of both of us if you just kept your mouth shut about this deer. This buck is going to be mine!" shouted Jasper.

Just then I saw headlights pulling into Jasper's driveway. It was Dad! I was so thankful to see him quickly getting out of his car.

"What's going on, Mason?" Dad asked.

"Nothing. He's just returning something of mine," Jasper said.

"What does he have of yours?" Dad asked.

Before I could say anything, Jasper was in the house, and all I could hear was the moaning of the old, rusty, screen door slamming behind him.

"Let's leave, Dad. I'm ready to go home," I said quietly.

I went over and opened the passenger side of the car. Inside I slumped in the seat.

"Is everything all right, Son? What did you have to return to Jasper in the middle of the night?" Dad asked.

I just sat in the car, silent. Dad stared at me. He could tell that I didn't want to talk about it.

"I guess it was a good night for me to go to town and get some milk for Mom. I'm only glad that on the way back I saw you on Jasper's front porch, and that you're okay, Boone," Dad said.

I was simply happy to spend some time with my dad—even if it was a short ride back home. To my surprise he didn't ask me again about what I was doing at Jasper's. When we got home, he saw me to my room and prayed with me. I couldn't help but hope that someday I was going to do something special that would really get my dad's attention.

I fell asleep ever so thankful I had made it off Jasper's land alive for the second time. The next morning, I was awakened by the sound of vehicles—a lot of them. I sat up and wiped my eyes. I looked out the window and saw two trucks driving up and down our road. Being on a dead-end road, we usually don't get much traffic.

Then the phone started ringing. I staggered out of the kitchen confused by all the commotion.

"Boone, I think you're famous," Rex said.

"What are you talking about? Famous for what?"

Rex held up the *Pikesville Press*, and I was on the front page in a huge picture—the picture that Mom had taken of Hank, Miles, and me holding the monster antler the night before. It took up half the newspaper page, and the photo was in full color.

The headline read in big, bold letters: "The Ghost Buck Lives in Pikesville!" At first, I smiled and thought it was pretty cool to have my picture in the paper.

But not everyone was happy with the picture.

-19-

There was a loud knock at the door. I had just finished breakfast, and my first thought was it was probably Miles stopping by to tell me that our picture was in the paper. I walked to the door and opened it.

I was surprised because it wasn't Miles. It was Jasper! His face was red, and I could see a small vein sticking out of his forehead.

"You couldn't leave well enough alone, could you?" Jasper yelled.

For a second, I just stood there—not really sure how to react.

It was kind of like the feeling someone would get when they're in class not paying attention and the teacher calls on them. I froze. Finally, after several seconds, I said the first thing that popped into my head.

"What do you mean?"

Jasper took a step closer to the door and said in a low, evil voice, "You think you're so smart. I already told you once that this buck was mine. I've been waiting a long time. You're not going to take this away—not you or your friends!"

I didn't even have time to explain. Before I could answer, he was storming off our porch heading for his old truck. As he was about to get in, he turned and shouted, "You know you couldn't ever shoot a buck like this. You'd just miss and ruin it for all of us!"

And with a slam of his rusty car door, Jasper was gone just as quickly as he'd arrived. While he left his tires spitting up the slushy snow, his parting words echoed through my mind.

I grabbed the paper and took one more look at the picture that had made me famous for all the wrong reasons. Now everyone knew the Ghost Buck was a world-class deer.

For some reason, the old man had known exactly what to say to keep my fears lingering in the back of my mind.

Ever since the first time I'd heard the story of the buck, a thought kept rolling through my mind: *Do I have what it takes to make the shot on the Ghost Buck?*

That thought scared me. It scared me even more than Jasper or Mumbles ever scared me. It was a thought that I was going to have to wrestle with—a thought that no one could help me with.

I knew it wouldn't come down to my new bow or my tree stand. Whether I ever bagged the Ghost Buck was going to come down to *me*.

-20-

The snowy winter had given way to spring, which had quickly turned into an early summer. Pikesville had now unofficially turned into a carnival. When I say *carnival*, I don't mean a fun place with exciting rides and cotton candy. I mean it was filled with a bunch of clowns. Everyone wanted a piece of the Ghost Buck, and most would stop at nothing until they found him.

Several well-known magazines had already visited and published stories on the mysterious buck. It was a story that was spreading like wildfire across the country.

Hunters from all around flocked to our tiny town, hoping to catch a glimpse of the Ghost

Buck. A lot of townspeople were happy, including Hank because these visitors were spending lots of money here. The downside was all the traffic and questions. I couldn't tell you how many times I had people ask me about the buck. I even had a guy offer me money to show him the exact spot where the shed was found.

I would always tell them that Hank was the one who had found the antler, not me. I was telling the truth because the antler in the photo was the one that Hank had found.

No one knew about the shed that I had found at Jasper's, and I wasn't going to tell anyone about it. I had seen how mad Jasper was and wanted to steer clear of any trouble. Plus, I didn't really want people to know that I knew the location of a second shed. The fewer hunters in our area, the better chance I had of bagging the buck.

Every morning at the Main Street Café, there was a new story about the Ghost Buck. Rumors started to spread, and everyone knew someone who claimed to have seen the monster buck.

One local claimed to have deer camera pictures

of the buck, but no one ever saw them. People in Pikesville were struck with big buck hysteria. Another person claimed that the buck had been hit by a car about two miles out of town, but I knew that the buck was still alive.

In my heart, I thought that there were too many things that had happened for this to be just mere coincidence. I knew that hunting this buck was part of my destiny.

I spent a lot of time that summer shooting my bow at targets. There was only one problem—I wasn't a particularly good shot. I couldn't seem to get consistent. I'd shoot and hit around the ten ring and then on my next shot almost miss the target.

I found it hard to shoot my new bow. This was my first compound, my first real bow. I had an old recurve that I had used around the yard when I was younger, but I didn't consider that a real bow. When I was younger, I was only shooting around the yard for fun, playing like little boys do.

This compound bow was real, and it was mine, and with it came a journey toward manhood.

-21-

"Hey, Dad. Is there any way you could help me with my bow today?" I asked during breakfast.

Dad was looking for his briefcase, tying his tie, and checking his email all at the same time.

"Sure, after work I'll go out and give you a couple of pointers," said Dad.

Years ago, my dad used to hunt quite a bit, but that was before he was promoted at work. Once he got the promotion, he seemed to have a lot less time for hunting and for me.

Grandpa would always say stuff to my dad about old hunting memories and all the great times they had together. Dad would always reply, "When things slow down, I'd like to get out in the woods again."

But those were just words. My dad was consumed by work, and it seemed like we were drifting further apart.

"I love you, Son," Dad said as he was walking out the door.

"Love you too, Dad. See you tonight. I'll be ready," I said.

"Oh, yeah, that's right, your bow. Yep, tonight I'll help you get that thing figured out," Dad said.

Dad's cell phone rang, and he was gone. I watched the dust roll off his tires as he drove down Wilderness Road. I told myself that this time he would make it home, that this was important to him too.

I waited all day. The sun started to set and go down for the night, and then the phone rang. My mom answered, and I knew who it was.

Mom talked for a minute and hung up the phone. She came into the living room and told me that Dad was on his way home. He was sorry for not being home early enough to help me with my bow, and he would try tomorrow.

The words were empty. I had heard them so many times.

That night I decided that I couldn't depend on my dad for any help. I knew I had to become a better archer. October was coming, and I had to be ready for anything, especially a shot at the Ghost Buck.

I knew exactly who to call—someone who would drop anything to help me with hunting. I called my grandpa, and, within two minutes of our conversation, we'd made plans. Tomorrow Grandpa was coming over.

By now the Ghost Buck was a well-known celebrity across the state. It was usually the topic of conversation whenever anyone came into Pikesville. Even though Grandpa lived an hour away from Pikesville, he knew all about it.

Everyone in his town talked about the buck. I hadn't had a chance to spend much time with him since Christmas, and boy, did I have a lot to tell him.

The next morning Grandpa pulled in around 9:00 a.m. I was looking forward to spending some time with him and having him help me with my bow.

I ran up and gave him a big hug.

"We got a lot of work to do today, Boone."

"I know we do. I can't wait!"

First, he wanted to see all my tree stands and walk the property. I was glad because this was the perfect time to tell him about everything that had happened during the past couple of months.

I told him all about Jasper and finding the shed antler. I also shared with him how I knew that buck was still around Wilderness Road. Most kids would be afraid to tell an adult stuff like that, but I knew Grandpa would listen. I also knew he'd believe me.

We walked around the property until we came to the back food plot, the one that was close to Jasper's property. I had freed Mumbles about two hundred yards from this spot.

"He's here all right, Boone," said Grandpa.

I stopped dead in my tracks. "Who's here?" I asked. For a second, I thought he was referring to Jasper.

"That buck...he lives around here. I can tell," Grandpa said.

For a second, I thought he was just saying that because I had told him about finding his shed nearby. Without saying a word, Grandpa pointed.

I couldn't believe my eyes, there were rubs on about six trees. These weren't your average buck rubs. They were huge! In fact, they went halfway up Grandpa's body. We walked over and admired them. Grandpa was even in shock at how big the rubs were.

"Boone, let's go practice shooting your bow," Grandpa said with a grin.

-22-

For some reason I was especially nervous as I put out the target. I had been shooting my new bow all summer, but as I walked back to shoot in front of Grandpa, it all seemed new again.

I really wanted to impress my grandpa.

I nocked an arrow, pulled up, aimed and shot. I barely hit the target. I grabbed another arrow, aimed, let go, and this time I hit the other side of the target—probably fourteen inches to the right of my first shot.

"See, Grandpa, something isn't right," I said frustrated.

"Shoot a couple more, Boone," Grandpa said.

So I did. Same result. I was all over the place.

Grandpa took a big breath and said, "I can fix it, Boone, but you're going to have to really listen."

"I will, Grandpa. Please help me."

Grandpa went on to tell me that it had nothing to do with my bow.

Nothing to do with my bow? I looked up at Grandpa with a dumbfounded look.

But as Grandpa spoke, it all started to make sense. He said, "Boone, you're doing a lot of things right when you shoot, but you don't have any faith. You need to trust in yourself and believe that you can make the shot. If you don't think you're going to hit the mark, then you won't. It's that simple."

Grandpa is right.

I always thought about missing instead of believing I was going to make the shot. It was like shooting a basketball and knowing that you were going to miss. His reasoning made perfect sense to me, but then a tough question popped into my mind—a question that I thought would even stump Grandpa.

"How do I fix that? How do I find faith?" I asked Grandpa.

"No one ever said trusting yourself is easy, but I know you can do it. You won't make the shot until you believe that you can do it," Grandpa explained.

"Is there anything I can do when I'm shooting that would help?" I asked.

I was certain Grandpa had some tricks up his sleeve—something from all his hunts.

"To be a good archer, you have to have rhythm. Everything needs to be smooth. I have a routine I follow every time I draw my bow. It's the same whether I'm shooting at a target or a big buck," Grandpa said.

I get it! It makes sense.

There was a verse from church that I loved. It always gave me strength. I nodded at Grandpa and grabbed an arrow. I was at full draw.

I took a deep breath and said, "I can do all things through Christ!" and released the arrow.

Bullseye!

I grabbed another arrow and went through the exact routine.

Bullseye!

Problem solved!

Grandpa looked at me and winked. "Now remember to do exactly what you just did because it will be a lot harder when you're staring at a monster buck," encouraged Grandpa. He added with a smile, "Harder, but not impossible."

He knew me well and always seemed to know what to say when I needed it the most.

-23-

It was late June, and school had just gotten out a couple of weeks earlier. Rex and I were already preparing for the fall hunting season. I spent a lot of time shooting my bow.

Miles was coming down today with his tractor to plow up and plant our two acres. Usually Hank did it, but since we were almost eighth graders and Miles worked on their farm anyway, Hank let him bring it down.

Dad would usually slip the Atwaters some corporate tickets to a professional basketball or football game for their help since we didn't own a tractor.

I was thankful for Miles' help, but more than anything, I wanted my dad to be home and help me with my bow skills. I was hoping maybe he'd even go hunting with me in the fall.

He wouldn't be around to help today, however. He had another big account meeting at work. I was sick of hearing about how important these meetings were. Supposedly he and his business partner, Jim Stewart, were working on some huge multi-million dollar deal with a Japanese company.

"Why can't Dad stay home from work just one time?" I asked my mom as I was walking out the door.

"Be patient, honey. When we first met, he loved to hunt and spend time in the woods around Pikesville. He and Grandpa were inseparable. But then your dad started working in the city, and his outlook changed. Don't give up on him; he does love you," Mom said.

"I know he loves me, Mom. That's not the point. It just seems like his boss, his job, and his clients are more important."

"Well, they're not. Maybe he just needs you to tell him how you feel, Boone."

Shaking my head, I left to meet Miles. *How*

could I tell my dad how I felt? I wondered. I didn't have the guts to do that.

Miles and I drove back to the first food plot. It was about an acre, and we were planting clover on it. We had two stands nearby—the Hotel and a new one we had just made and named the Cedar. The Hotel was a big wooden shack on stilts that Rex always sat in during firearm hunting season. The new stand was a ladder stand that we had named the Cedar. It was located between two large cedar trees that provided perfect cover.

The ground worked up well, and Miles was quickly off to plow up the second food plot near Jasper's property line. This was the spot that I had dreamed about hunting for so long because I knew it was special.

The loud noise of the tractor came to a screeching halt. The next sound that I heard was Miles' yelling.

I took off running and was out of breath when I finally reached him. My jaw dropped open, and I could hardly believe what I saw. Near three old cedar trees was the biggest scrape I had ever seen.

Both Miles and I were speechless as we went over to it. The ground foliage had been cleared away, and even though the season had ended earlier that year, we could still make out a huge area that had been used as a scrape. Bucks use scrapes to communicate with other deer. This scrape told me that the Ghost Buck had spent some serious time on our land in the past year.

"This wasn't here last hunting season. I'm sure of that," I said to Miles.

"Boone, it might have been, and you just missed it," Miles said.

"How did we miss something this big?"

Maybe Miles was right. It could have been made during the last part of the rut last year.

It was in a peculiar spot—one that you would have to walk around some other trees to see. The spot was perfect for a buck hoping to leave his calling card.

I wasn't sure when it was made, but it was definitely a buck's scrape. And I knew there was only one buck that could make a scrape like that.

-24-

Miles set the drags on his tractor and began slowly working the food plot. I was walking around picking up rocks so they wouldn't get caught when I heard the familiar sound of Jasper's four-wheeler.

The noise got louder. The next thing I saw was the old man standing against his ATV on the property line staring at us. He must have heard Miles screaming about the buck scrape, or he might have just been patrolling his property as he did on a regular basis.

I waved, but he didn't. He just stared. His was a cold blank stare. Miles noticed him and gestured for me to go talk to him. I shook my head and told him to do it. He acted like he couldn't hear me and kept working the field.

The field was almost completely worked up when I heard a loud noise. It was a weird sound. It reminded me of the sound a baseball bat makes when it hits a ball. It was a short, loud sound that even got Miles' attention. Miles had hit a huge rock. He shut off the tractor, and I went over to investigate. On my way over, I heard an even more disturbing sound.

It was the sound of laughter, but it wasn't a normal happy laugh. It was Jasper, and he was laughing very loudly. I stopped and looked at him. I couldn't help myself. I was sick of this old man. I couldn't let him get away with mocking us anymore.

"What's so funny?" I yelled.

After I spoke, I knew I should have kept my big mouth closed because now he was mad. I don't think he liked a young kid snapping at him.

Jasper stopped laughing. "I'll tell you why I'm laughing, boy. I think it's funny that you two kids are getting your property ready as if you're going to get a buck. I don't think you even got the guts to shoot one, kid!"

I didn't know how to respond. Doubt started

to creep in, and I wondered if he was right. I had never killed a buck—let alone one the size of the legend I was chasing.

Luckily, the next noise I heard was the sound of the four-wheeler, and Jasper was gone—gone like a bad dream. The thoughts he left behind were like a nightmare that would haunt me.

I knew Jasper would still be around watching and waiting for me to screw up.

-25-

The summer seemed to have stalled. Most kids love summer vacation, and I usually did. But that all changed when I became obsessed with the story of the Ghost Buck.

I couldn't wait for school to start again because that meant it was fall. The hunting season couldn't come fast enough. It was now early August. I had spent a lot of my summer daydreaming about bowhunting the Ghost Buck.

Miles and I did a lot of fishing in Catcher's Creek too. The large creek—about fourteen feet wide—snaked its way through everyone's property on Wilderness Road. We had two spots where we liked to fish. The first spot was located on the

Atwater's farm, and the other spot was where the creek cut through our property.

One particular morning, we decided to fish the hole on our property. Miles met me at my house in the morning and grabbed a shovel. We often dug for big night crawlers that we used as bait on our fishing adventures.

We went behind the garage to a spot that used to be a garden. Mom hadn't had planted a garden in years, but it was the perfect place to find worms. I dug the shovel in and scooped out a load of fertile, black dirt. There were about ten night crawlers in the first scoop.

I took another scoop and found a couple more. Just as I dug my shovel into the ground for a third scoop, Miles grabbed my arm. I looked up and could see that he was staring at something in the woods. For a second, I didn't see anything. Then I caught movement behind a tree. It was a buck!

We watched as the deer fed on some acorns as it moved through the woods. It was a nice sixpointer. We were both excited.

"That was awesome!" Miles cried.

"Wow! Did you see his horns? They were still in velvet. That was a big buck, Miles!"

Since neither one of us had ever shot a buck, we thought it was a giant. As we sat admiring the buck feed, we saw him stop and look. *There's more deer!*

We sat quietly and watched as another buck—a spike—took the same trail as the six-point. It seemed to catch up as they both ate acorns and scratched about, looking for more.

We were just about to get back to digging worms when we saw one more deer coming. The deer had its head down, but we could tell it was noticeably bigger than the other two. The hide was also peculiar. It seemed to have more of a grayish tint.

The buck slowly picked his head and looked toward us. It was him—the Ghost Buck. He was even bigger than I had ever imagined.

Suddenly the huge buck was gone. I was so glad that Miles was with me, or I might have thought I had seen a ghost. We both sat silent for a couple minutes.

"Do you still want to go fishing?" Miles asked.

"No, I think I'm going to go practice shooting my bow."

-26-

There were no more sightings of the huge buck the rest of the summer.

September arrived, and that meant we were back in school. I was nervous about being in the eighth grade, but it helped that it was almost hunting season.

In Michigan, we have a special youth hunting season the last weekend of September. Youth hunters are allowed to use either bow or gun during this special season.

Even though I could hunt with a gun, I chose to use my bow instead. Ever since I had gotten it on Christmas Day, I had my mind made up that I would use it to get my first buck. Since I was only

13 years old, the law said I had to have someone over 21 go hunting with me.

Dad and I had made plans to hunt on Saturday morning. We couldn't hunt Friday because he had to work late. When I got home from school, I spent hours organizing my hunting gear. I couldn't stop my mind from racing, so I double- and triple-checked my hunting gear. I wanted everything to be perfect, just like I had planned it for so long. Saturday morning couldn't come fast enough!

When I finished packing my gear, I grabbed my bow and practiced. With Grandpa's help, I had gotten rather good over the summer and felt confident shooting.

When I was done, I went inside to call Miles. I knew Miles and Hank were going out in the morning, so I wanted to wish them luck.

"Hey, Miles. Are you excited?"

"We sighted my gun in tonight, and I'm ready," said Miles.

As I hung up, I couldn't help but wish Dad would have been home with me, so he could've seen me shoot my bow.

When Dad got home around 9:30 p.m., I was waiting for him in the kitchen.

"Hey, Dad. Glad you're home. We got a lot to get ready for tomorrow."

He walked over to the fridge and poured a glass of orange juice. He took a drink and looked at me. I knew right away that something was going on. Mom could tell too.

"Honey, what's wrong?" Mom quickly asked.

"It's the Furikawa account. I don't think we're going to get it. I think we lost it. They're going to go with someone else," Dad said.

Dad seemed defeated, which was odd for him. He was usually so positive, so energetic. I could tell this was a big deal.

"Are you sure? Have they already decided?" Mom asked.

"Not yet, but it doesn't look good," Dad said.

Then he looked at me. Deep down I already knew what he was going to say before the words trickled out of his mouth. They felt like tiny knives poking at my soul.

"Boone, I'm not going to be able to take you

hunting tomorrow. I have to work on that account to see if I can save it. I'm so sorry," said Dad.

I already started walking to the phone. I knew someone who would drop everything to go hunting with me.

Grandpa and I excitedly made plans for the next morning.

-27-

It was finally here—the day I had been waiting and planning for all summer. It was Opening Day.

I got up really early—way before sunrise. I couldn't sleep any later. I got dressed and tried to eat a little cereal. I couldn't eat much and found myself trying to create deer antlers from my breakfast cereal.

My excitement level rose even higher when I saw the headlights of Grandpa's truck pulling in. I jumped up, grabbed my gear, and headed for the door.

As I was leaving, I stopped one more time to see if my dad was up. He wasn't, but I knew he would be soon because he had to be at work again.

I hesitated a moment but decided I wasn't going to wait for him anymore. I had to be the one to make this hunt happen.

I gave Grandpa a hug, and we went out into the dark towards the back food plot. We climbed up and settled into the Eiffel Tower.

The slow sunrise started to shed light onto the food plot and surrounding woods. I felt Grandpa give me a nudge.

I turned as he pointed to a deer moving through the woods in our direction. I started to tremble. I felt a hand on my shoulder, and I turned to look into my grandpa's gentle, smiling eyes and started to relax.

When I saw horns, my heart instantly flipped over. It was a buck, and he was coming right toward us!

As it got closer, I could tell it wasn't the Ghost Buck, but it was a nice six-point buck. I could hardly contain myself. I was going to take a shot if it came close enough. I had made up my mind last year that I would shoot the first buck that I had a chance at. Even though I had decided this before I heard of the Ghost Buck, I wanted to stick to my word. Nothing is easy about getting a buck, especially with a bow and arrow. I was thankful to have a chance at my first one even if it wasn't the Ghost Buck.

The deer started to head away from us. I started to get worried. It didn't look like I was going to get off a shot. Just then, the buck stopped and turned back to our location.

I grabbed my rangefinder and put it on the buck. It read 18 yards. I drew my bow and tried to slow my breathing. I put my 20-yard pin on the deer, which was now standing broadside. I took one easy, steady breath and pushed my release.

And I missed...

-28-

I turned to look at my grandpa and tried not to tear up. I was so disappointed. The confidence I had gained by practicing all summer was gone in an instant. I looked at my bow and then examined my sight. I was trying to find an excuse for missing the target, but there wasn't any. Missing the buck was my fault.

"What happened?" I asked Grandpa looking for answers.

He sat quiet for a minute and took a long breath.

"Buck fever happened. Boone, you just missed. It happens to everyone. You didn't hold the shot. You peeked to see where you hit. Your arrow went underneath the buck," he said.

It was true. I had looked to see where my arrow was going to hit.

We waited for another couple hours and didn't see any more deer. I was glad we didn't see anything else. My confidence was so low that I didn't feel I could hit anything.

As we walked up to the house, we were both quiet. I kept looking at my sight and my bow. I was looking for answers in the wrong spot. Usually, Grandpa has to quiet me down in the woods; this time I wasn't saying a word.

Just as we made it to the backyard, I heard a nearby gunshot. It was on the Atwater farm. Miles had taken a shot!

I took off my hunting gear and threw it in the corner of the garage. I grabbed the phone and called him, but no one answered.

Mom had lunch ready for us, but I barely ate. I mostly just picked at it. Finally, we jumped in Grandpa's truck and headed down the road to investigate the shot we'd heard.

Did Miles miss too? I had only heard one shot, but maybe he got one. Did he shoot the Ghost

Buck? I tried to convince myself to be happy for him. The truth was that I would be devastated. Not only did I miss a buck, now the buck I had been dreaming about and preparing for could be gone. My only solace was the fact that it was Miles. I would rather have had Miles shoot the buck than Jasper.

We pulled up to the barn and saw a big deer hanging from the rafters. I took a deep breath and put on a smile.

As we walked up, Miles saw us and came running. He was grinning from ear to ear. He was breathing heavy with excitement when he finally reached us.

"Boone, I got him!" screeched Miles.

I didn't know what to say. I looked at Grandpa. He was speechless too. I gave Miles a hug and walked into the barn to see the giant that had haunted my dreams.

-29-

Wow! What a buck! It was huge. His antlers almost touched the rafters of the pole barn, and the deer had a big, thick neck.

But it wasn't the Ghost Buck.

I did feel some guilt about wanting the Ghost Buck all to myself, but I managed to smile for Miles.

"It has eight points!" Miles proclaimed. I looked the buck over, and it was definitely a trophy.

Hank stood in the barn, smiling proudly at his son.

"The buck's spread is eighteen inches wide. I know it's not the Ghost Buck, but it doesn't matter to me!" Miles declared.

We took pictures and listened to the story of how he had shot the deer. They had seen a couple of other bucks but had no sightings of the mysterious buck we were all after.

I was too embarrassed to tell him about my buck, the one that I missed. I started thinking that maybe I should have used a gun, but that thought didn't last long. I was on a mission and wanted to get a buck with my bow. Besides, with the crummy way that I was shooting, there was no guarantee that I'd be able to hit a deer with a gun either.

Grandpa had to get home, so I thanked him, and we said our goodbyes. Just as he began to drive away, he stopped and rolled down his window.

"Boone, remember everyone misses. I know what a good shot you are with your bow."

I nodded and walked into the house. I had thought I was ready. If anything good did come out of missing, I told myself that I'd never peek at the shot again.

The Youth Hunt ended. I didn't have a buck.

Now I had to wait another week before it was October 1—the opening day of archery season in

Michigan. At least no one else had killed the Ghost Buck. If they had, it would have been in all the newspapers and even on TV. It wasn't, but some nice bucks were taken.

Two things made hunting difficult. The first was school. By the time I got off the bus and changed, it was late. The last thing I wanted to do was scare deer away from my stand. That limited me to only hunting on the weekends.

The second thing was that I always had to have an adult with me. The fact that I had to depend on my dad to be able to hunt drove me crazy. Trying to get him to take time to go hunting with me was almost impossible, so much so that I finally stopped asking.

Grandpa and I would go out on Saturday mornings together, but that only gave me one chance a week to hunt.

October came and went, and suddenly it was November. I was starting to get nervous because gun season was only weeks away. I knew that if I didn't get the buck before gun season, I was in big trouble.

Everyone, and I mean everyone, gun hunted in Pikesville. It was the second week of November, the last Saturday I could bowhunt before the firearm season opened.

That's when everything changed.

-30-

Grandpa had called the night before to tell me about a cold front moving in and a chance of snow. It wasn't going to be a lot of snow but just a dusting that would cover the ground. This cold weather would get deer up and moving. And just the week before, he had noticed several scrapes around the food plot.

The rut season was on, and the bucks would be moving!

I was up early and ready when Grandpa pulled in our driveway. He was bundled up in warm clothing and had some sort of backpack with him. I didn't ask him any questions. I just figured if Grandpa was bringing it, there had to be a reason.

It had snowed the night before just like the forecast predicted. Sometimes we get snow in November but usually not until after Thanksgiving. It was a welcome sight and made the ground glow a dazzling white.

Because of the snow, it took a lot longer to get back to the Eiffel Tower. We were both careful to step slowly and cautiously over twigs and branches. The last thing we wanted was to spook any deer off the food plot.

When we got to the tree, I bent down, clipped my bow to my pull-up string and started to climb up the ladder stand. After about three steps, I had a strange feeling and stopped climbing. I turned and Grandpa was gone. For a second, I freaked out! I started looking around in the darkness and finally found his silhouette. I got down and went over to him. "Grandpa, what're you doing?" I whispered.

"I'm helping you find your faith," Grandpa said.

Without saying another word, he reached into his bag and pulled out a ground blind. He started to set it up. I helped him, and in a matter of minutes, the blind was up and ready.

I unzipped it and started in when Grandpa grabbed my arm.

"This isn't for you, Boone. I'll be right here watching everything. You need to finish what you started—by yourself!" Grandpa said.

A cold chill went through my body. At first, I thought it was the north wind that had been blowing, but it wasn't. It was fear.

Grandpa was right. I needed to do this on my own.

I climbed up and took my spot in the tree stand. I glanced back at Grandpa, and he nodded. I nodded back.

It was cloudy so it took a long time for it to get light, longer than usual. The sun finally peeked out from behind the clouds, and the forest woke up. Birds started chirping, and I heard a flock of geese fly overhead.

I was listening to the birds singing their magical song when a strange crunching sound caught my attention. I couldn't place exactly where the noise was coming from, so I started scanning the woods.

The sound was getting louder and louder. I

grabbed my bow and got ready. *Squirrel.* I let out a big sigh. It was a big fox squirrel collecting nuts for the long winter ahead. I started laughing to myself at how that little squirrel got my blood pumping.

About a half hour later, I heard more crunching. This time it was heavier—a different sound. I turned. It was a deer, and it was getting close! I froze. Almost to my relief, it was a doe. She walked out into the food plot and started milling around.

Seconds later, I heard more crunching coming from the same spot where the doe had emerged from the trees.

I looked back and saw HIM!

-31-

HE WAS HUGE!

As soon as I saw his rack, I had to make myself concentrate solely on his body. I wanted to focus on where I needed to make the shot. The doe had moved into the food plot and was feeding directly in front of me. He was right on her trail with his head down.

I reached for my rangefinder but couldn't grab hold of it. I was shaking too much. It was only a matter of seconds, but it seemed like everything began to happen in slow motion.

Slowly the enormous buck turned and looked right up toward where I was hiding. *Has he somehow spotted me?* If I moved an inch, the buck sure as anything would bolt, and I'd lose the opportunity of a lifetime. Tense seconds ticked past. Then the buck looked back down.

Now was my only chance. I told myself, Don't peek. Hold the shot. I didn't want to make the same mistake I'd made earlier on the six-point. My mind flashed back to the summer—to the buck I had missed and my other misses.

Not this time, I told myself. *Not anymore!*

As I drew my bow, my thoughts centered on all the good shots I had taken. I knew I was going to hit this buck. My life had been full of misses but not today. Today was my day. I went through the same routine I did when I was shooting with Grandpa.

I silently said my verse, almost like a prayer: *I can do all things through Christ who strengthens me.*

I took a deep, calming breath and released the arrow.

-32-

I had no idea where I hit the giant, but I knew I had hit him. I had heard a loud "whack," but in the excitement of the moment, I wasn't sure where the arrow had landed.

I was shaking so badly. My excitement quickly turned to worry as I tried to climb down from the stand. It was difficult to do as I tried to force myself to relax to avoid an accident. I finally reached the ground and unhooked my safety harness.

I went over to Grandpa. He had not seen the shot, but he did see the buck as it ran away, and he knew for certain that I had hit him. I have never seen Grandpa smile so big. He was jumping up and down, pumping his fist. We walked over to the spot where the buck had been standing. There was no blood, and we could not find my arrow! Since we didn't know where the arrow had landed, we decided to pull out and head back to the house.

It was around 7:45 a.m. as we started to walk back. I kept replaying the shot in my mind. After a year of stories and dreams, I had only seen the monster buck for a matter of seconds.

We finally made it back to the house and burst in the door.

"I hit him!" I yelled.

Rex was at the table eating, and Mom was in the kitchen, finishing making pancakes. My dad was starting to put on his suit jacket, getting ready to leave for work.

Everyone stopped what they were doing and stared. They could tell by the look on my face that I was serious. I quickly told them the story of my encounter with the Ghost Buck. I even got Dad's attention.

Rex was the first to say something.

"Let's go find him," said Rex quickly.

Wow! Even Rex is excited for me.

Just as Dad started to say something, his cell phone rang. It was Jim, his business partner. I knew whenever Jim called, it was a big deal.

"Hello? Did you set up the meeting? What time? I'm on my way," Dad said.

How could Dad leave for work today? I walked over to the sink so no one would see my watering eyes. Dad came toward me and put his arm around my shoulders.

"That's right, Jim. I'm on my way—on my way to track my son's buck. I won't be in to work today. You're going to have to take care of the meeting," Dad said.

I can't explain the excitement in my heart when I heard Dad utter those words. I had waited so long to hear him choose me. And he had!

"I need to start heading home. Grandma is waiting for me," Grandpa said with a wink.

I knew—we all knew—what he was doing. His work was done; I had my dad now.

I thanked him with a hug. As he went out the door, I couldn't help but be thankful for Grandpa's time and wisdom.

Rex and Dad changed their clothes and put on their boots. We walked out the door a team. It's hard to explain the feeling of going with my dad and brother back into the woods that day. I was overwhelmed with emotion, but there was still one unanswered question.

Was the Ghost Buck dead?

We approached the food plot, and I pointed out my tree stand and where I thought the buck had been standing. We started to look around for some evidence of the hit, but we weren't finding any.

"Boone, why don't you climb back into your tree stand just to make sure we're looking in the right spot," Dad said.

Once I was sitting in the Eiffel Tower, I knew right away we hadn't been looking in the right spot. I told Dad and Rex to move about fifteen yards to the west of where we had originally been looking. They moved, and I started to climb back down the tree.

Just as I had reached the last step, I heard Rex shout, "I found some blood!"

We went over, and sure enough, there There

was no mistaking the pin-sized drop of blood on an oak leaf. I had hit the Ghost Buck!

We started to slowly track the blood drops. We got on our hands and knees, looking for even the smallest drop. We spread out about ten feet apart, working our way back and forth looking for blood. Whenever we found a new drop, Dad would stay on the last one while Rex and I worked our way ahead.

Every time we found more blood, I would get even more excited. We tracked the buck for about 100 yards until we couldn't find another trace.

We started to circle the area and found where the buck had turned.

His track was so unique that we could spot it right away. The buck turned to the north and was heading right for the thicket at the back of our property. We began tracking him again right through the thicket by following his blood trail.

Then we all stopped. We still had a good trail, but there was a major problem. The buck had crossed over and gone onto Jasper's land. A huge cloud of depression fell over all of us as we stared at the old fence line that separated the two properties. I could tell Dad was trying to think of what to do next.

Should we just keep tracking the deer, grab him when we found him, and drag him back without the old man knowing? I thought to myself. I could tell that Dad and Rex were thinking the same thing.

After a couple minutes, Dad finally spoke up, and I couldn't believe what he said next.

-33-

"Let's go talk to Jasper," Dad said.

What? Go talk to the person who patrols his land every night? Jasper is the same guy who could probably win a place in the *Guinness Book of World Records* for the number of No Hunting Signs on his property.

"Dad, are you sure? What if he says no and keeps the buck for himself?" asked Rex.

Even Rex isn't sure if that is the best idea!

"We're going to have to take that chance," Dad responded.

With our heads held low, we reluctantly walked back through the woods to our house. The walk back was much different than when we had excitedly set out to look for the buck. No one talked, and there was a dark mood over all of us.

Could the buck be gone forever?

We loaded into Dad's car and made the quick drive to Jasper's house.

I stared out the window, wondering and hoping for a miracle. We slowly rolled into Jasper's driveway.

"Let me do the talking, Son. Jasper can be tough sometimes," Dad said.

I nodded. I knew from firsthand experience that I didn't want to talk to Jasper. I wanted Dad to take care of this. I wanted him to protect me. All three of us walked up the porch.

Dad knocked on the door. Then the barking started, and we waited for him to answer the door.

When the door creaked open, Jasper was standing with Mumbles at his side. Dad kept trying to talk, but Mumbles was barking too loud. Finally, Jasper yelled to quiet the dog.

"What do you want?" Jasper demanded.

"My son hit the big one. He hit the Ghost Buck this morning. We tracked the buck for a while, but he crossed onto your land. I know how you feel about people being on your land, but that's Boone's buck," Dad said.

A sense of pride filled me. My dad was there for me, defending me.

As the old man listened to my dad, we could tell he was disappointed but surprisingly not angry.

"He hit him? He arrowed the giant?" Jasper finally asked.

Just then Mumbles started barking again, ripping at the door. At first, I thought he was trying to go after my dad, but it was a different kind of bark. Jasper yelled, but the dog kept barking.

"What is it, boy?" Jasper asked and opened the door.

The dog ran out and headed past Jasper and my dad and right toward me!

"Watch out, Boone!" Dad yelled.

-34-

As the dog was barreling toward me, my dad tried to go after him, not knowing that Mumbles was now my friend. When the dog reached me, he laid down on his back, and I bent over and started scratching his belly.

I could tell my dad and Rex were in awe.

They had never seen Mumbles as anything but a mean, nasty dog.

"Boone, what in the world…" said Dad in bewilderment.

Jasper stood there just shaking his head.

Feeling empowered by my new status, I asked Jasper, "So you think we can go after the buck on your land?"

"I suppose just this one time," Jasper relented, but then he added, "Only under one condition."

"Anything," my dad responded.

"Can I go with you? I want to see the buck one last time."

Dad and I just stared at Jasper.

"What do you mean?" I finally spoke up and asked.

"We have a history together," Jasper said, and he began to talk about the buck.

It was strange to hear Jasper talk about the Ghost Buck. For the first time I saw Jasper in a different way. He wasn't the mean old man that we had known for so many years. He was a fellow hunter—someone who appreciated the animal he was pursuing. We had something in common—we had both been obsessed with the Ghost Buck for the past year.

Jasper went inside to grab his coat and joined us on the porch. While we all headed toward the woods together, he began to tell us about his encounters with the buck over the past year. Evidently, he'd seen the buck several times and was fairly sure it was living in a certain section of his woods. Then I remembered something.

"Is that why you drove around your property every night?"

"I became so obsessed with the giant, I wanted to keep him on my property so I could have him all to myself," Jasper admitted.

"A buck like that could do that to anyone, Jasper," my dad quietly said.

The old man just nodded in reply.

-35-

We walked the fence line back to the spot where the big buck had crossed it. We had left Rex's blaze-orange stocking cap where we had found the last blood. Dad bent down and showed Jasper.

"I think Boone must've hit the liver," Jasper said. "How long ago did it happen?"

I looked at my watch. It was 7:20 a.m. when I first looked at my watch after shooting the buck. Now it was almost 1:00 p.m., so we had given the buck about five and a half hours.

I told Jasper and he nodded, almost reassuring me we had taken enough time before looking for the giant. After tracking for about 50 yards, we found a spot where the buck had lain down.

"You probably jumped him when you were tracking him the first time," Jasper said.

I started to get nervous. With a hit like that, you have to give the deer plenty of time. Eventually, he will lie down, but if you push too fast, you could lose the buck.

Thankfully, we found more blood and continued to track another thirty yards. But that was it. We finally ran out of blood.

We divided up and slowly, methodically circled the area, looking for any further sign. With every passing minute, I grew more disappointed. It wasn't looking good.

My worst fear was starting to become reality. I had a chance to get the legendary buck and blew it. My greatest worry was wounding the giant and losing him forever.

Dad and Jasper began talking as if they were ready to give up when I heard a low distant barking. Jasper heard it too.

It was Mumbles.

We all exchanged glances, and, without a word, started running toward the barking. He was down by the creek about eighty yards from where we were all looking.

Rex and Dad were the first ones there. I was next, followed by Jasper. Once I reached the riverbank, I saw Rex and Dad silently staring at the edge. I ran toward them and suddenly saw him. The buck was lying on the edge of the river. I started to cry. I couldn't help it. This deer had done something special for me.

I felt a cold hand on my shoulder.

"Good job, Boone. You deserve that buck," the gruff voice said.

I turned to thank Jasper and hugged the old man. I had a feeling that the events of the past year had changed his life too.

Jasper hiked back to his house to retrieve his four-wheeler. Even with four people, the buck was way too big to carry out. Eventually, we got him back to our house. I was numb; it all felt like a dream. My mom grabbed the camera and snapped pictures of all of us with the Ghost Buck. We even convinced Jasper and Mumbles to be in a couple of pictures.

Just when I thought the day couldn't get any better, Dad turned to me and said, "Hey, Boone, do you want to go to the archery shop with me tomorrow afternoon so I can get a bow too?"

I smiled. In that moment, life felt much different to me. For the first time in a long time, I believed in myself...and in my dad.

About the Author

LANE WALKER is an award-winning author, speaker and educator. His book collection, Hometown Hunters, won a Bronze Medal at the Moonbeam Awards for Best Kids Series. In the fall of 2020, Lane launched another series called The Fishing Chronicles. Lane is an accomplished outdoor writer in the state of Michigan. He has been writing for the past 20 years and has over 250 articles professionally published. Walker has a real passion for outdoor recruitment and getting kids excited about reading. He is a former fifth grade teacher and elementary school principal. Currently, he is a Director/Principal at a technical center in Michigan. Walker is married with four amazing children.

Find out more about the author at www.lanewalker.com.